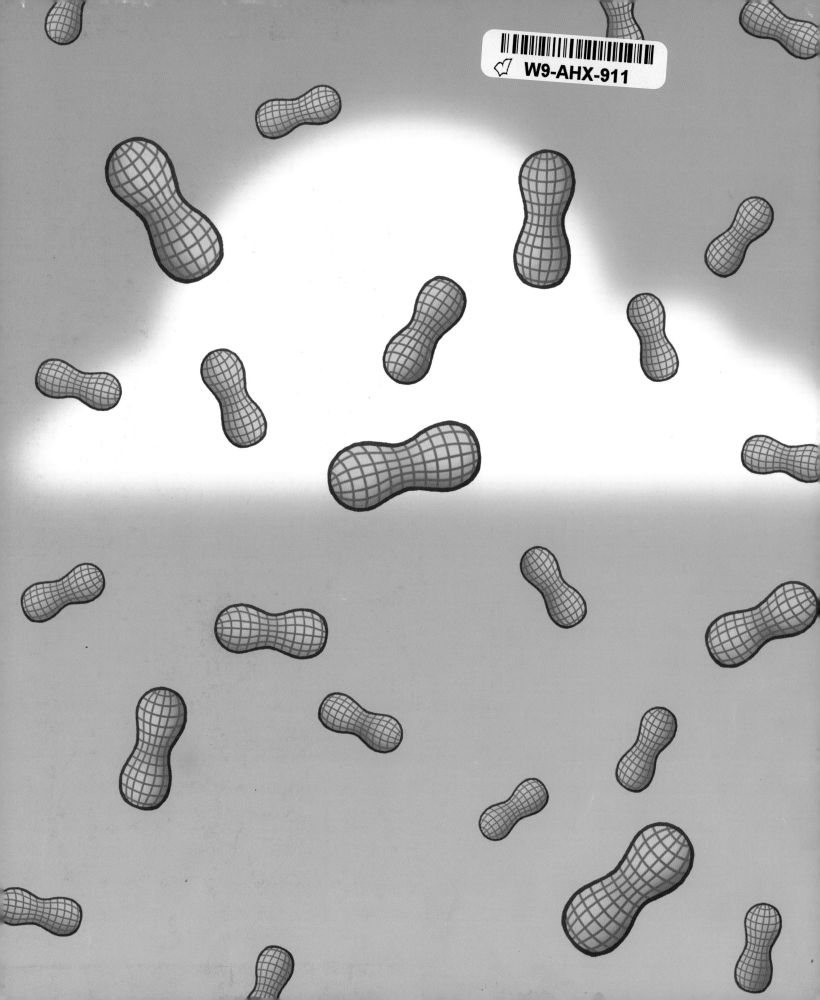

For the assorted nuts
in my family,
Cheryl, Mason, Sloane, & Paxton.

A special thanks to Connie & Paula
for helping me cook up the idea for this story.

A FEIWEL AND FRIENDS BOOK
An Imprint of Macmillan

Printed in April 2010 in China by Leo Paper, Heshan City, Guangdong Province.
For information, address Feiwel and Friends,
175 Fifth Avenue, New York, N.Y. 10010.

Library of Congress Cataloging-in-Publication Data Available

ISBN: 978-0-312-54967-1

Book design by Michael Wright and Kathleen Breitenfeld

The text type is set in 25-point Hank.

Feiwel and Friends logo designed by Filomena Tuosto

First Edition: 2010

10 9 8 7 6 5 4 3 2 1

www.feiwelandfriends.com

JAKE

GOES PEANUTS

By Michael Wright

FEIWEL AND FRIENDS
NEW YORK

Jake always gagged on carrots,

and he hated lima beans.

His mother's
tuna casserole
would haunt him
in his dreams.

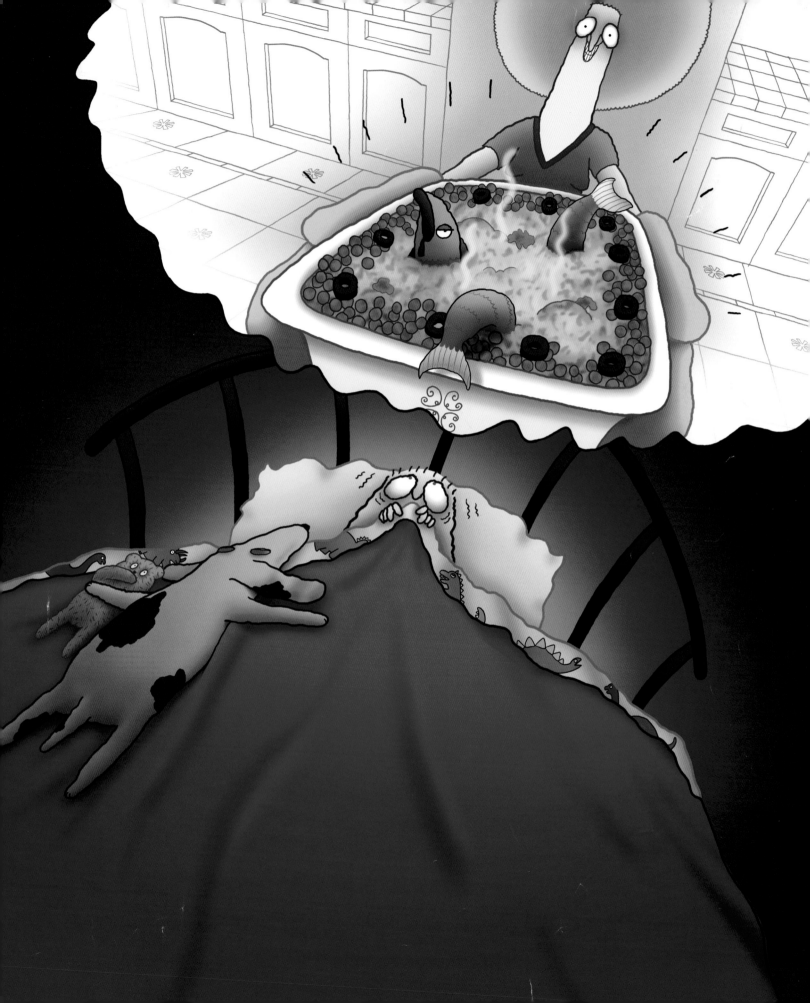

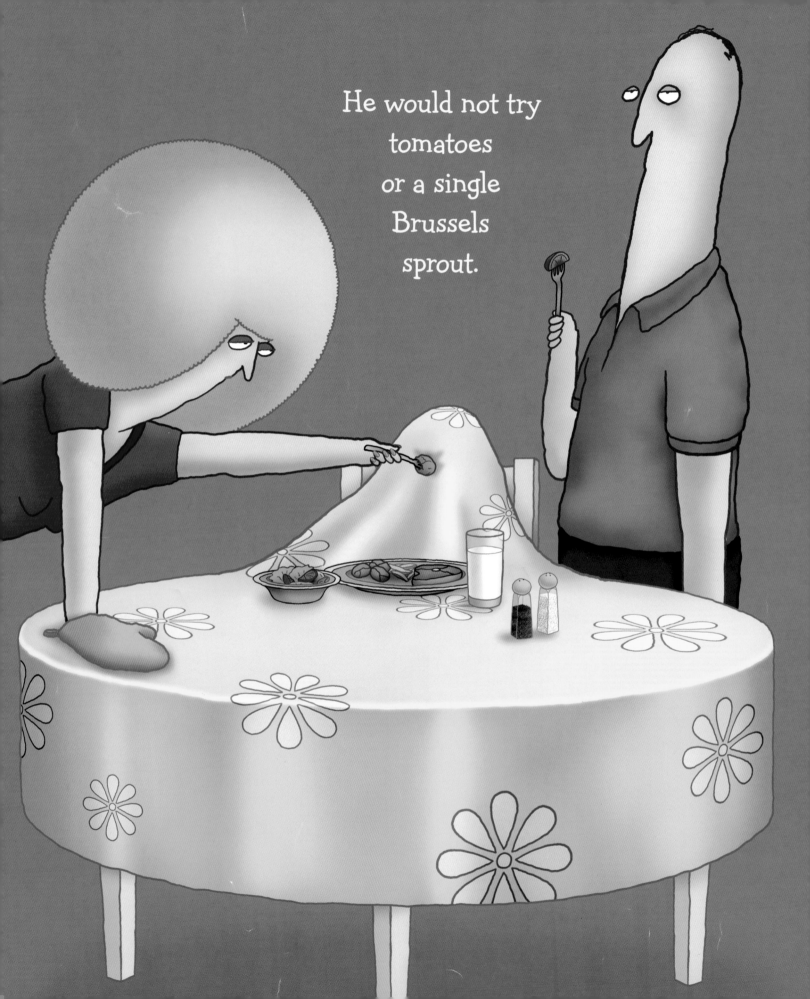

He would not try
tomatoes
or a single
Brussels
sprout.

So many items made Jake's list
of foods he would not eat.
But there was one thing he enjoyed.
It made a meal a treat.

A peanut butter sandwich,
no food could quite surpass.
Unless, of course, you teamed it with
some cold milk in a glass.

It wasn't long before that's all Jake ever would request.

For breakfast, lunch, and dinner, he simply liked it best.

His parents tried fresh recipes,
but nothing seemed to work.
Whenever they served something else,
their boy would go berserk.

When Jake strolled down to breakfast
and climbed up in his seat,
he asked his parents for another
"You know what" to eat.

FRED

Jake thought that didn't sound too bad and said . . .

They brought out peanut pancakes.
Jake devoured every one.
Then, smiling to himself he thought,
"Oh, won't this week be fun!"

They had peanut butter pot roast
served with peanut butter rice.
They had peanut butter soda
chilled with peanut butter ice.

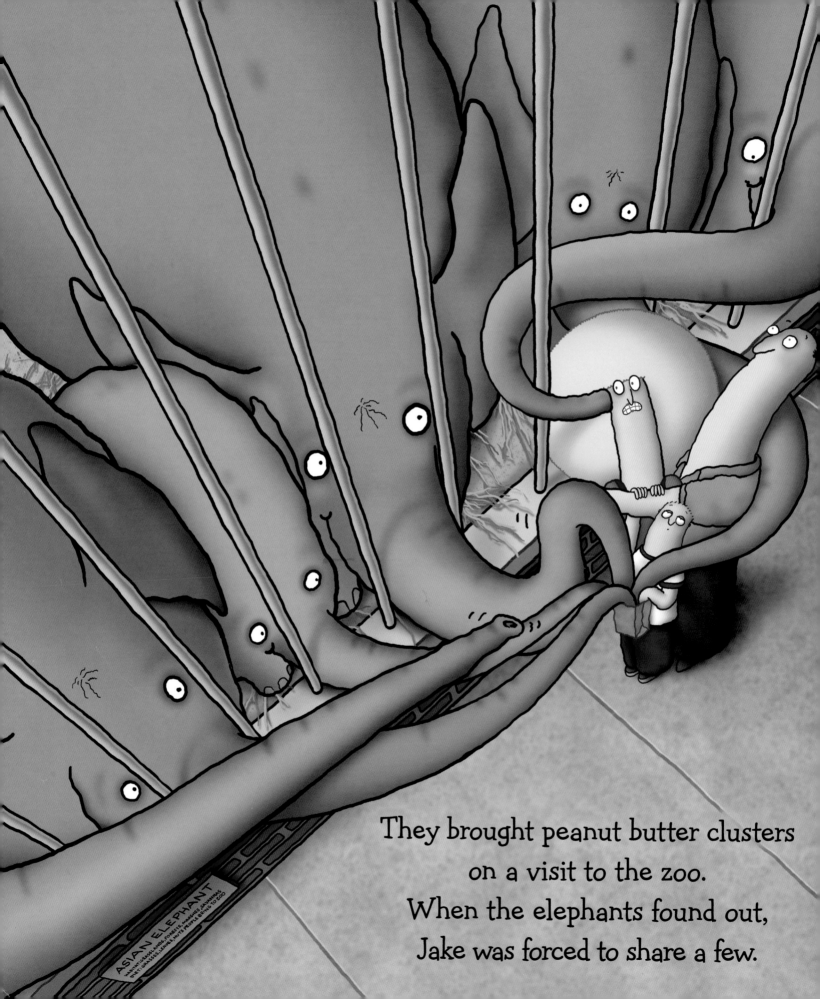

They brought peanut butter clusters
on a visit to the zoo.
When the elephants found out,
Jake was forced to share a few.

They ate peanut-stuffed roast turkey
at his grandpa's house one night.
That got the old guy sleepy
and he conked out like a light.

They even made some peanut butter
dog food just for Fred,

who slurped one bite and promptly got
his dish stuck to his head.

At school Jake knew that
there were kids
with peanut allergies.
He'd see them eat
the weirdest stuff
like sandwiches with cheese.

Jake much preferred his tasty lunch of peanut butter boats.
And as he picked one up he thought, "I wonder if this floats?"

Then he imagined sailing off
to Peanut Buttertown,
a far-flung place where everything
was peanut butter brown.

Where peanut butter waterfalls
spilled down from peanut skies,
and happy peanut people
led their nutty little lives.

One afternoon
they had a peanut picnic at the lake,
but discovered bugs love peanut butter
just as much as Jake.

As Peanut Butter Week wore on,
the peanut butter flowed.
Jake was surprised to find his love
for peanut butter slowed.

They dipped peanut butter crackers in their peanut butter soup.

Jake was eating
so much peanut stuff,
he made
peanut butter poop.

Halfway through the final meal
of Peanut Butter Week,
Jake put his fork down on his plate.
Then he began to speak.
"I think I'm sick of peanut butter.
I've had all I can take."

Now that Peanut Butter Week
has come and it has gone,
Jake's started trying different foods
he's missed for far too long.

Like crunchy orange carrot strips
Mom cuts in silly shapes.
Jake thinks they're fun to snack on
with a bowl of juicy grapes.

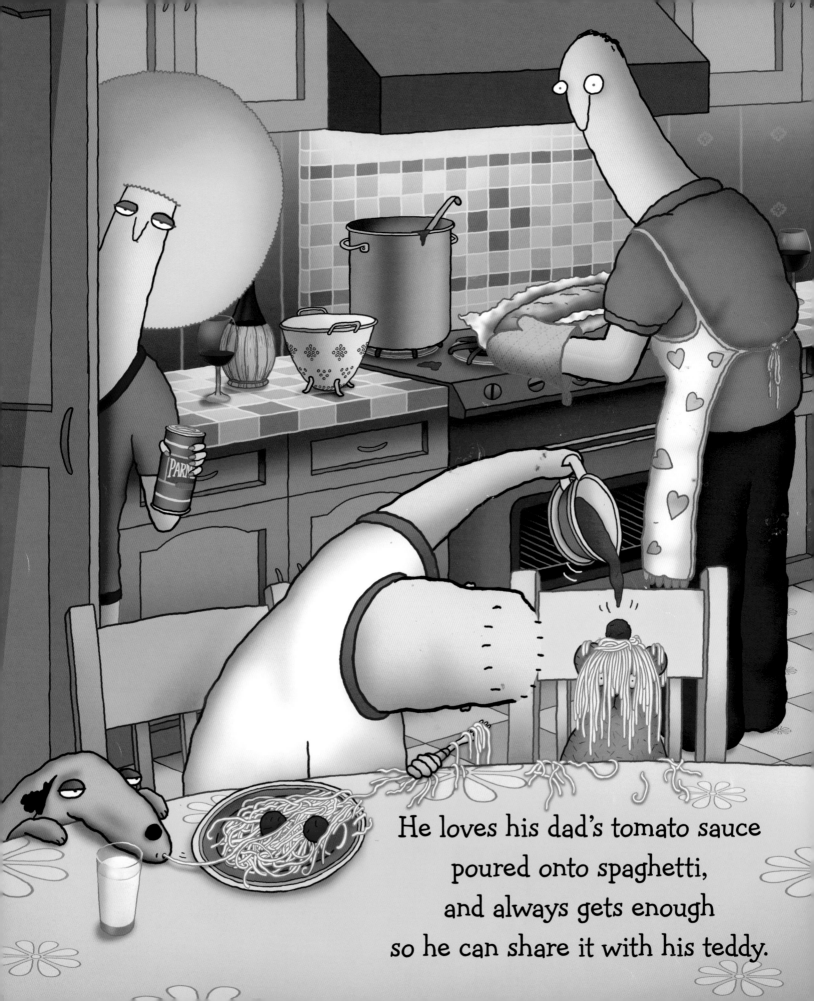

He loves his dad's tomato sauce
poured onto spaghetti,
and always gets enough
so he can share it with his teddy.

His parents are delighted Jake is eating like he should . . .

but his mother's tuna casserole
still isn't any good.

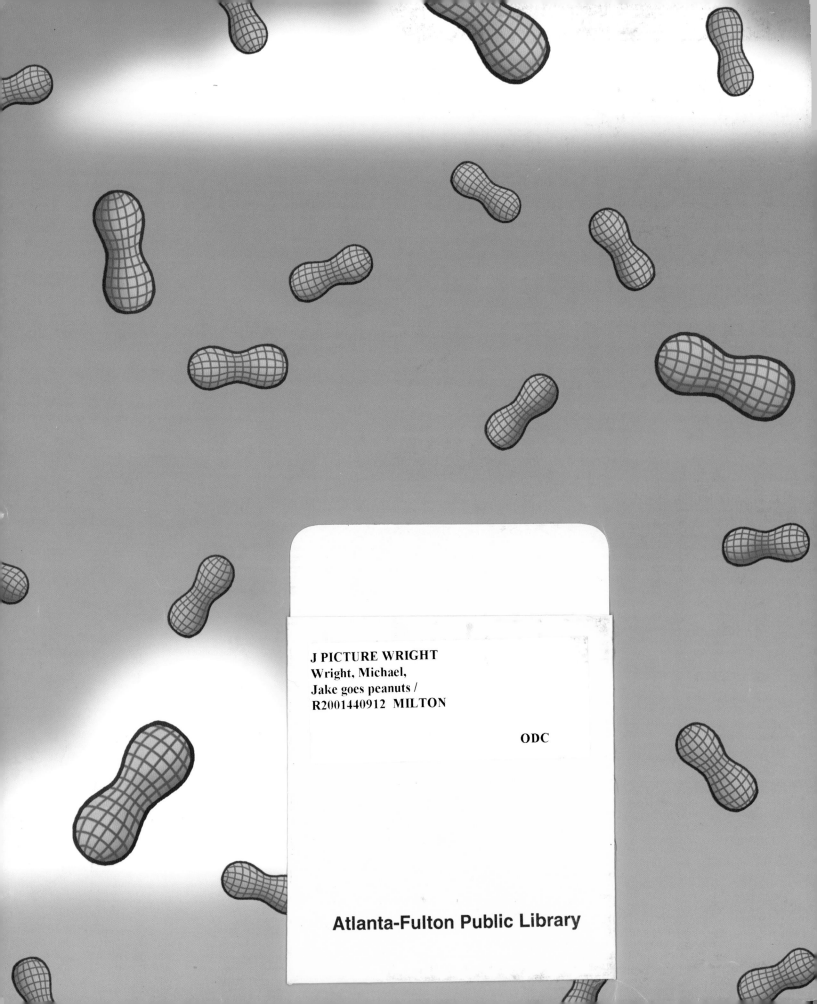